The Case of the
Kidnapped
Cupid

ISBN-13: 978-0-545-06686-0
ISBN-10: 0-545-06686-7

12 11 10 9 8 7 6 5 4 3   11 12 13 14/0

Printed in the U.S.A.

Book design by Jennifer Rinaldi Windau
This edition first printing, January 2009

Catch all of the Calendar Club Mysteries!

For Larry, with love
—N.S.

For my parents
—D.S.

The Case of the
Kidnapped
Cupid

by Nancy Star

Illustrated by Dan Santat

SCHOLASTIC INC.

New York   Toronto   London   Auckland   Sydney
Mexico City   New Delhi   Hong Kong   Buenos Aires

CHAPTER ONE
Neighborhood Watch!

Dottie Plum got to the clubhouse first.

Dottie liked to do everything first. But she especially liked to be first when it was her turn to check the Calendar Club Help Box.

The Help Box sat outside the front door of the clubhouse. And anyone in Fruitvale who had a problem could slip a note inside.

Dottie and her best friends, Casey Calendar and Leon Spector, took turns checking the box every day. Today was Dottie's turn.

Casey and Leon ran past Dottie into the clubhouse. Dottie's uncle Eddy had asked the Calendar Club to help make valentines for his store and they had agreed. Casey and Leon were eager to get back to work.

Uncle Eddy sold plants and fruit in the summer. He sold pumpkins in October. In February, he sold Valentine's Day flowers.

The three friends had been working on Uncle Eddy's valentines for nearly a week. They had already cut out the hearts and pasted on the cupids. All that was left to do was to print the message:

Won't You Be Mine?
Stop by Eddy's Store for
a free Valentine's Day chocolate rose!

They had promised to deliver the valentines to their neighbors as soon as they were done. And that was going to be today.

Casey and Leon sat down on the clubhouse floor and started writing the message on each valentine.

Outside, Dottie reached into the Help Box.

"We got a note!" she called as she joined her friends.

She tore open the envelope. "It's from Officer Gill!"

Dottie read the note out loud:

"Dear Calendar Club,

Miss Duffy has been away for more than a month. Can you keep an eye on her house for me? She lives in the ivy-covered corner house on Daisy Lane.

Your friend,

Officer Gill"

The three friends looked at one another. They were very good at keeping an eye on things. But they did not like the idea of keeping an eye on the ivy-covered corner house. They did not even like to walk in front of that house.

The ivy-covered house was almost always dark. The woman who lived there was hardly ever home. When she was home, she hardly ever came outside.

Dottie, Casey, and Leon couldn't be sure she didn't like kids. But they were pretty sure. And they didn't want to take any chances.

But they also didn't want to disappoint Officer Gill.

Dottie took a small notebook out of her back pocket. She carried her notebook wherever she went. Inside, she kept lots of lists. Her favorite list was of the weather.

Today, her weather list said, is forty-five degrees and cloudy.

Dottie started a new list called: Miss Duffy's House.

"Now I have a place to write things

down," she said. "In case we see anything unusual."

But even talking about the house made them nervous. So they went back to work on the valentines.

Finally, they finished and set out to deliver them. They took turns putting the valentines in their neighbors' mail slots. Dottie went first.

They were across the street from the ivy-covered house when Leon stopped. "We don't have to deliver a valentine if no one's home, do we?"

Before anyone could answer, a red convertible pulled up in front of the house.

A man hopped out. He wore a black sweatshirt and black pants that were streaked with pale gray paint.

A woman got out next. She wore a dark velvet coat with a thick fur collar. Her shoulder-length, wavy blond hair was as shiny as gold. She wore sunglasses even though it was a cloudy day.

"She looks like a movie star," Dottie whispered.

The woman opened the trunk of the car and struggled to take out a large suitcase.

"Why did you bring your whole dressing room with you?" asked the man.

"Who are they?" Casey whispered to her friends.

The woman yanked until she got the suitcase out of the trunk. Then she carried it up the steps of the ivy-covered house.

The couple got to the front door. The woman put the bag down and searched for something in her purse.

"I've never seen either of them before," Dottie said.

She opened her notebook to the list marked, Miss Duffy's House. She wrote:

Two people drove up in a red car.

The man whispered to the woman. She turned and looked at the three friends. And she smiled.

"She smiles just like a movie star," Dottie whispered.

"The man said she took her whole dressing room with her," added Casey. "She must be a movie star. They're the only ones who have dressing rooms, right?"

Dottie nodded, and added to her list: Woman has golden hair and probably is a movie star.

"Do you think she's famous?" Casey asked.

"I think we should call Officer Gill," Dottie said. "He wanted us to keep an eye on the house, remember?"

"Look," Leon said. "She has a key!"

Dottie and Casey looked. The woman

had just taken a key out of her purse.

"Why would a movie star have a key to Miss Duffy's house?" Casey asked.

"Maybe she's a relative," Dottie said.

"Maybe she doesn't know Miss Duffy is away," Leon said.

"I'll tell her," Casey said. She ran up to the woman before her friends could stop her.

"Excuse me," said Casey. "Did you come to visit? Because the person who lives here isn't home."

The woman who looked like a movie star smiled again, showing off her perfect teeth.

"That's so sweet of you to tell me," the woman said kindly. "But the person who lives here is home. You see, I'm the person who lives here now."

"You are?" Casey asked.

The woman nodded. "The lady who used to live here moved away. I'm sure she's very sorry she didn't get a chance to say good-bye."

"She is?" Casey said.

The woman nodded again.

"Do you live here, too?" Casey asked the man.

"No," the man said. He laughed and rubbed his nose.

Casey noticed that his hands had gray paint all over them.

"This is Howard," the woman said quickly. "He's my painter."

"Is that why your hands are gray?" Casey asked.

"You're a smart one, aren't you?" Howard said. He turned to the woman. "Do you want me to come in with you?"

"No," the woman said. "I'll call you when I'm ready."

"Okay." Howard winked at Casey and ran back to his car. Then he hopped inside and drove away.

The woman put her key into the lock. But it wouldn't turn.

"New keys are such a bother, don't you think?" she asked.

She tried the key again, jiggling it a few

times. Finally, it worked.

"There we go," she said as she opened the door. "Thanks so much for stopping by. But I've got a lot of unpacking to do. We can talk later, okay?"

She didn't wait for an answer. She walked into her new house and shut the door.

"I can't believe Miss Duffy moved away!" Dottie said.

"I can't believe a movie star moved in!" Casey said.

"We don't know that for sure," Leon reminded her.

"But I'm sure we can find out," Casey said. "Let's go!"

CHAPTER TWO
A New Friend

The three friends quickly delivered the rest of the valentines. Then they went to Casey's house to call Officer Gill so they could report what they'd seen.

The policeman who answered the phone explained that Officer Gill wasn't there.

"Can you tell him the Calendar Club called in with a report?" Casey asked.

"Sure thing," the policeman said.

Casey hung up the phone, and the three friends headed to her backyard.

"Why don't I just ask her if she's a movie star?" Casey said as she walked inside the clubhouse.

"We can figure out if she's a movie star without asking her," Dottie said. "We just have to think about the clues."

She opened her notebook and started a new list: Clues About Our New Neighbor. Number 1: She arrived on Wednesday.

"What else do we know about her?" Casey asked.

"Not much," Dottie admitted. "We don't even know her name."

"Can I draw a picture of her in your notebook?" Casey offered.

Casey wasn't a great artist, but Dottie didn't mind. She handed over her notebook. Casey started drawing.

"Hey, Leon," Casey said. "Did you notice what her suitcase looked like?"

Leon didn't answer.

"Leon?" Casey said again.

Casey and Dottie looked around the clubhouse. But Leon was nowhere to be seen.

This was nothing new.

Leon was a collector. His most important collection was of rocks that were in the shape of states. Leon hoped someday he would have an entire map of the United States made out of rocks.

But looking in rock piles, snow piles, and puddles often made him late.

"Leon!" Casey shouted.

Leon came running inside.

"Sorry," he said. "I thought I found a rock shaped like Arizona. I really want to find Arizona by Saturday."

"Why?" Casey asked. Leon had never mentioned Arizona before.

"Because Saturday is Valentine's Day," Leon explained. "And in 1912, on Valentine's Day, Arizona became the forty-eighth state."

"Is Arizona called the Valentine State?" Casey asked.

"No," Leon said. "It's called the Grand Canyon State."

"That's a good nickname, too," Casey said. And she went back to drawing.

Leon glanced at the notebook. "Who is that?"

"It's our new neighbor," Casey said. "Dottie doesn't think I should ask her any more questions so I'm drawing her instead."

"I just don't think we should go ringing doorbells for no good reason," Dottie said.

Casey stopped drawing. "I just thought of a really good reason!"

CHAPTER THREE
A Good Reason!

Casey's mother agreed. She would make a tray of brownies, and the three friends would deliver it to their new neighbor.

Mrs. Calendar owned a bakery, which was called Sweetie Pie, in Fruitvale. And her double-fudge brownies were everyone's all-time favorite.

Dottie, Casey, and Leon set off for the ivy-covered corner house as soon as the brownies were ready.

Dottie walked her cat, Ginger, on a leash. Ginger was a cat that thought she was a dog.

Casey came next, pulling her red wagon. A tray of double-fudge brownies sat inside, bumping along as they went.

Casey's dog, Silky, followed behind the wagon. Silky was a dog that thought he was

a cat. His favorite activity was sitting on a chair near the window, watching the world go by. Silky didn't like to go out for walks. But when he did, he hardly ever wore a leash.

Leon came last. He had fallen far behind to stop to examine a rock.

It wasn't what he was looking for. He tossed it back in the dirt and ran to catch up.

The three friends were almost at the corner when a delivery truck pulled up in front of the ivy-covered house.

They watched as a deliveryman carried a big box to the front door. He rang the bell. The door opened. He handed the box to someone inside. Then he went back to his truck and drove off.

"Come on," Casey said. "The movie star is home." She ran to the front door and rang the bell.

A moment later the movie star opened the door.

"Well, hello there," she said. "To what do I owe this unexpected pleasure?"

Casey wasn't sure exactly what that meant. But she figured that was how movie stars talk.

"We have a club," Casey explained, as she handed the woman the tray of brownies. "It's called the Calendar Club. We figure things out. And we figured out you like brownies."

"How did you know about my terrible sweet tooth?" the woman asked. "Thank you so much." And without another word, she smiled and closed the door.

"Why didn't she invite us in?" Casey asked.

"I guess she's too busy to talk to us right now," Dottie said.

"Still," Casey said. "If it were me, I

would have invited us in."

Ginger stepped toward the front door and pushed it with her nose.

"See?" Casey said. "Even Ginger wants to go in."

Ginger pushed a little harder. The door hadn't been closed all the way. It opened a few inches.

Dottie held back on the leash so Ginger couldn't open it any more.

But Silky wasn't on a leash. And now Silky was interested in the door, too.

"Want to go in the house?" Casey asked Silky.

Silky always liked being inside better. He wagged his tail, and slipped through the narrow opening.

"Silky!" Dottie called out.

Casey smiled. "I guess we better go get him."

For once, Dottie was glad she wasn't first.

CHAPTER FOUR
A Real Collection!

Casey pushed open the front door the rest of the way. It made a loud groaning sound. She took a step back.

Casey didn't scare easily. But they had been afraid of the corner house for a long time. And the house was still a little scary, even without the scary woman in it.

"Hello?" Casey said. She walked inside.

She turned and motioned for her friends to follow her.

Reluctantly, they did.

"Anybody home?" Casey asked.

"We know she's home," Dottie whispered.

"We just saw her," Leon whispered.

"I know," Casey whispered. "But you're still supposed to say 'Anybody home?' when you walk into someone's house."

"Anybody home?" Casey asked again.

The three friends stood in the front hall. Casey glanced up at a giant crystal chandelier that hung from the ceiling.

"That looks like something from a movie," she said.

"So does this," Dottie said. She walked over to a giant mirror that filled up half a wall. "She's definitely a movie star. No one else would have a mirror this big."

Dottie and Casey looked in the mirror and noticed Leon wasn't with them.

"Leon?" they whispered.

"I'm in here," he whispered back.

They followed Leon's voice into the living room.

"Look at that!" he said, pointing to a table.

Dottie and Casey looked. On top of the table there was a collection of rocks.

The rocks were all different colors — red, yellow, rusty orange, and blue. A light on the wall was pointed right toward them, as if the rocks were in a museum exhibit.

"She's a movie star who collects rocks!" Leon said.

"And globes!" Dottie said. She walked over to where three antique globes sat on wooden stands of different heights.

"Rocks and maps!" Leon said.

They heard a distant bark.

"Silky!" the three friends said together.

They ran down a long hall until they reached a room that looked like a library.

Bookshelves jammed with old books lined three of the walls. Against the fourth wall was a huge display case. It had a glass front and was filled with statues.

They heard another woof. Silky scurried out from behind a big box.

"Silky!" Casey exclaimed.

The movie star stood up from where she had been crouching behind the box.

She looked surprised to find that she had guests.

"How did you get in?" she asked.

"Your front door wasn't closed all the

way," Dottie explained.

"And Silky ran in," Casey said, as her dog rubbed against her leg.

"So we had to come in to get him," Leon said.

"We're very sorry," Dottie added.

"Sorry?" the movie star said. "I think Silky is the cutest dog I've ever seen. He just might be the cutest dog in the whole wide world. And I would know," she added, "because I've traveled the whole wide world."

Dottie, Casey, and Leon's eyes got wide. They had never met a movie star before. And they had never met anyone who traveled all over the world.

"Is that why you have so many globes?" asked Casey.

The movie star looked surprised.

"I saw your rocks," Leon said. "I collect rocks, too."

"You do?" she said.

Leon nodded.

Just then Silky barked, and ran back to the box.

Casey followed him. She stopped to examine the box. It had airmail stickers all over it.

"Did this come from far away?" she asked.

"Yes," said the movie star.

Casey peered inside the box. But all she saw was crumpled newspaper. "What was in there?" she asked.

"Just a little doodad I picked up for myself when I was in Paris," the movie star said. "That's in France," she added.

"We know," Leon said.

"But we've never been there," Dottie said.

"I've never even been on a plane," Casey said. She looked in the box again. "Can we see the doodad?" she asked, even though she didn't know what a doodad was.

"And after we see it we'll leave," Dottie said, because she was starting to feel as if the movie star wanted them to go.

"I'm awfully busy right now," the movie star said.

"Just a quick look?" Casey asked. "Please?"

It was hard to say no to Casey.

"All right," the movie star said. "As long as it's quick."

She went behind the box and lifted up the package she had been unwrapping when they arrived. It took several minutes to pull off the remaining layers of newspaper and bubble wrap. It was more bubble wrap than any of them had ever seen before.

When she was finally done, the movie star lifted out a small white statue.

"It's for my garden," she said. "It's a cupid. Isn't he cute?"

"But it's broken," Leon said, pointing to where an arm was missing.

"It was made that way," the woman said quickly. "So that it looks old."

"The broken arm must be the one cupid used to hold his bow and arrow," Dottie said.

"You're a very bright little girl," said the woman.

"Why do you collect cupids?" Casey asked.

She had wandered to the display case and noticed that all the statues inside were cupids.

"Cupids, maps, and rocks!" Leon said.

The woman laughed.

"Where did you get all of these statues?" Casey asked.

"I'd love to tell you," the woman said.

"But I still have a lot to do. Can we talk some other time?"

"Sure," Dottie said. "Come on, Silky," she called.

"Can Leon look at your rock collection before we go?" Casey asked.

"Or we can come back later," Dottie said.

"Later sounds good," the woman said.

"What time later?" Casey asked.

"How about if I give you a call?" the woman said.

"That would be great," Dottie said. She pulled Casey along with her as she started walking out of the room.

Casey stopped. "Don't you want a phone number?"

"Of course," said the woman. She went to her purse and searched for something to write on. She pulled out the top part of a flyer that had been ripped in half and turned it to the blank side.

"Here you go," she said, handing it to Leon. "You can write down the number for your club right here."

Leon took the paper. "Our club doesn't have a phone."

"Do you want him to write down his home number instead?" Casey asked.

"Divine," the woman said.

Dottie, Casey, and Leon weren't sure if that meant yes or no.

The woman noticed their confusion.

"Tell you what," she said. "I'll call you first thing tomorrow morning, and you can come right over then. All right?"

"Okay," Casey said.

But as soon as they got to the sidewalk, Casey stopped.

"Wait a minute," she said. "We can't go over tomorrow morning. We have school."

"That's okay," Leon said. "She's not going to call, anyway."

"What do you mean?" Casey asked.

He held up the paper the woman had given him. It was still blank. "I never got a chance to give her my phone number."

"I don't think she wanted it," Dottie said.

The three friends walked home in silence, each of them wondering why.

CHAPTER FIVE
The Wrong House!

The next morning they set out for school. Casey led the way. Dottie walked behind Leon, recording the day's weather in her notebook as she went.

They were almost at the corner when Leon stopped suddenly to pick up a rock. It wasn't what he wanted. He stopped again to put it down. That's when Dottie walked into him.

The books and papers they were carrying to school went flying in all directions.

It took several minutes to pick them up. They had just finished when the morning newspaper was delivered to the front lawn of the ivy-covered house, across from where they stood.

"Let's wait and see if the movie star comes out to get her paper," Casey said.

But Leon was starting to feel uncomfortable. "The house looks very dark," he said.

Dottie felt uncomfortable, too. "It looks like no one's home."

"Do you think she might be out making a movie?" Casey asked.

Just then a big black limousine turned onto their street.

"That looks like a movie star's car," Dottie said.

The car pulled up in front of the ivy-covered house and stopped.

A passenger got out of the back. But it wasn't the movie star.

Dottie was the first one to recognize her.

"It's the woman who used to live there,"
she whispered. "It's Miss Duffy."

The black car sped away.

Miss Duffy walked to the front door of
the house.

"Do you think she forgot that she doesn't live here anymore?" Casey whispered.

Miss Duffy took out her key. She put it in the lock. But when she tried to turn it, it didn't work.

She looked around, puzzled. Then she saw the three friends watching from across the street.

"Come on," Casey said. "Let's go!"

They ran all the way to school. And they never looked back.

CHAPTER SIX
The Broken Lock

They tried not to think about Miss Duffy during math or social studies or art or gym. But it was hard.

Finally, the school day was over. Dottie, Casey, and Leon hurried home. But when they turned onto Daisy Lane, Leon stopped.

"Look!" he said, pointing.

Casey and Dottie looked. Officer Gill's car was parked in front of the ivy-covered house.

The front door of the house opened. Officer Gill and Miss Duffy walked out.

"Good morning," Officer Gill called over.

"Solve any mysteries today?"

"No," Casey said. "Did you?"

"I'm just here to help Miss Duffy," said Officer Gill. "She came home and found her front door lock was broken."

Dottie, Casey, and Leon were surprised that Officer Gill didn't know Miss Duffy had moved away.

"That lock was stuck the other day," Casey said.

"How do you know that?" Miss Duffy snapped at her.

"I asked the Calendar Club to help me keep an eye on your house," Officer Gill explained.

"But how would she know the lock was stuck?" asked Miss Duffy. "Unless she was the one who broke it."

The three friends took a step back. They didn't want to make Miss Duffy angrier than she already was.

"Did you sneak into my house while I was away?" Miss Duffy asked.

"Hold on, now," said Officer Gill. "I've known these young people for a long time. And they are not the kind of kids to sneak into an empty house. I'm sure of that. And I'm sure they have a very good explanation for how they know the lock was stuck." He turned to them. "Don't you?"

Dottie nodded. "We were here watching the house the day the movie star moved in."

"What movie star?" Miss Duffy asked.

Casey turned to Officer Gill. "Miss Duffy doesn't live here anymore. A movie star lives here now."

"We're not positive she's a movie star," said Dottie.

"But she definitely told us she lives here now," Leon said. "And that Miss Duffy moved away."

"I didn't move away," said Miss Duffy. "I was in Paris working on a story."

"Miss Duffy is an investigative reporter for a very important newspaper," said Officer Gill.

"When did you meet this movie star?" asked Miss Duffy.

Dottie took out her notebook and checked.

"It was Wednesday," she said.

Officer Gill took out his notebook and started to write that down.

"I think I'd like to get my notebook, too," said Miss Duffy.

"Why don't we talk about this inside?" suggested Officer Gill.

Everyone agreed. And Dottie, Casey, and Leon followed Officer Gill and Miss Duffy back inside the scary house.

CHAPTER SEVEN
What's Missing?

Miss Duffy got her notebook and sat down next to Officer Gill on a long sofa.

Dottie, Casey, and Leon sat facing them on deep chairs in front of a big, stone fireplace.

Officer Gill took out his pen.

Dottie and Miss Duffy took out their pens.

"What made you think this so-called movie star was moving in here?" asked Officer Gill.

"That's what she told us," Leon explained.

"She had her own key," Casey said.

"And she brought lots of beautiful things," Dottie said. She looked around the room. "She brought those rocks and those globes."

Miss Duffy interrupted her.

"This is my globe," she said quietly, as she walked over to the biggest globe. "These are my things. I've spent years collecting them from around the world."

"Is the rock collection yours, too?" Leon asked.

"Yes," said Miss Duffy. "Those are pieces of petrified wood. I got them as a gift many years ago when I was doing a story about the Petrified Forest."

"You went to the Petrified Forest in Arizona?" Leon asked.

"Yes," said Miss Duffy. She sounded impressed that he knew where it was. "It's one of my favorite national parks. It's got fossils that are millions of years old. Have you been there?"

"No," Leon said. "But I want to go."

"He's very interested in rocks," Dottie explained.

"And in Arizona," Casey added.

"I'm interested in all the states," Leon said.

"Have you been to lots of different states?" Casey asked.

"Not lately," said Miss Duffy. "Lately I've been traveling all around the world."

"That's what the movie star said," Dottie remembered.

Miss Duffy narrowed her eyes. "Who is she?"

"I think we'd better take a walk through your house and make sure nothing is missing," said Officer Gill.

Miss Duffy thought that was a good idea.

She took her time looking around the living room. "Everything here seems to be fine."

They followed her through the rooms on the first floor. Nothing looked out of place. Finally, they got to the library. Miss Duffy hurried over to the glass case to check the statues.

"I'm so glad the cupids are all here," she said.

She sounded relieved. But Dottie looked worried.

"Something is different," Dottie said. "Something is definitely different."

She spotted a wastebasket in a corner of the room and walked over to it. She peered inside.

"Bubble wrap," she said as she pulled out a large sheet of it from the wastebasket.

"And newspaper!" Casey said, spotting a ball of bunched-up newspaper under a small desk.

Leon found the empty box. It had been flattened and shoved between a small couch and the wall. He pulled it out.

"That's the box the doodad came in!" said Casey.

"She means the garden statue that was delivered while you were away," explained Dottie.

"It was a cupid," Leon said. "And it was broken on purpose to make it look old."

Miss Duffy turned pale. She sat down on the small couch. "Was the cupid missing an arm?"

"Yes!" Dottie said.

"That woman is no movie star," Miss Duffy said. "She's a thief — a very clever thief. And that statue is very valuable. It was made by a talented sculptor more than a hundred years ago."

"Who sent it here?" Casey asked.

"The owner of the statue. He's a friend of mine," said Miss Duffy. "He lives in Paris. He was helping me with a story I've been

working on for months. I've been tracking a gang of international statue thieves."

"We write about thieves, too!" Dottie interrupted.

"We have a newspaper called *The Monthly Calendar*," Casey said. "Did you ever read it?"

"No," said Miss Duffy. "But I'd like to." She smiled.

The three friends thought Miss Duffy didn't look at all scary when she smiled.

"But why did your friend send the statue here?" asked Casey.

"The statue thieves pretend to be art experts," Miss Duffy explained. "People hire them to figure out what their statue is worth. The thieves have workshops in cities all around the world. They offer to take the statue to their workshop to examine it. But the statue they return isn't the same one they picked up."

"They make fake statues!" Dottie said. She was writing in her notebook as fast as she could.

"That's right," said Miss Duffy. "And the fakes are very good. Most people don't even know they've been robbed. My friend was trying to catch them. He invited the thieves to take a look at the statue and tell him what it was worth. But first he made his own copy of it. He sent the original to my house for safekeeping."

"Did his fake statue fool the thieves?" Casey asked.

"They never showed up," said Miss Duffy. "Someone tipped them off."

"Is that why you came home?" Casey asked. "To find them?"

"No," said Miss Duffy. "I came home to return the one-armed cupid to its owner."

She turned to Officer Gill. "I never got a chance to see the thieves myself. But that woman must be one of them. I don't know how she found out that I had the statue, or how she got a key to my house. But I have to find her. I have to get that statue back."

"Don't worry," said Dottie. "The Calendar Club is on the case!"

CHAPTER EIGHT
Gray Is Clay!

The three friends agreed to meet back at the clubhouse later that afternoon.

Dottie got there first.

Leon got distracted by a rock, so he came last. It was his turn to check the Help Box. He stuck his hand inside and pulled out a note.

He ran inside the clubhouse and read the note out loud:

"To my dear Calendar Club,

If you think of anything that might help me find those awful thieves, please stop by my house, anytime, day or night.

Your Friend, Miss Duffy"

"Why did we think she didn't like us?" asked Casey.

"I can't remember," said Dottie.

"Neither can I," said Leon.

"We've got to help her," said Casey. "But how?"

"Maybe there's something we forgot," said Dottie. "Something obvious. Something right in front of our eyes."

Leon stood up. "Or in our pockets," he said.

He reached into his pocket and pulled out the torn piece of paper the movie star had given him. The crumpled paper was blank on one side. But Leon turned it over. The other side was part of a flyer. He read what was printed on it: "Stella Gallery. Specializing in Art and Antiquity."

"Who's Aunt Iquity?" Casey asked.

Leon didn't answer. "Look." He pointed to the bottom of the paper. "It says 'Nicole and Howard Blank.' "

"Howard was the name of the movie star's painter," Dottie said.

"Remember how his hands were covered with gray paint?" Casey asked.

Leon's eyes got wide. "I just thought of something else that can make hands look like they're covered with gray paint. Something we used in school today."

"Clay!" Dottie and Casey said together.

"That was dried clay on his hands," Dottie said. "Howard must be the one who makes the fake statues!"

"And if Nicole is the woman we thought was the movie star," said Casey, "she must be the brains of the operation."

"Look," Leon said, pointing to the bottom of the paper. "You can see part of their phone number written here."

"Too bad it was torn," Dottie said. "Now we can't read it."

Leon reached his hand into his other pocket and pulled out another piece of paper. It was very small.

"Maybe we can," he said.

"What is that?" Casey asked.

"I picked this up by accident," he said, "when Dottie and I crashed into each other and dropped all our things."

He put the pieces of paper together, like a puzzle. And they fit!

"It's the phone number," he said.

"We still don't know if the movie star is Nicole," said Dottie.

"But I know how we can find out," Casey said.

She ran out of the clubhouse. Dottie and Leon followed her. By the time they caught up to her, she was on her kitchen phone. She had already dialed the number.

They huddled close to listen. The phone rang for a very long time. Finally, someone answered it.

"Stella Gallery," a woman's voice sang out.

"That's her," Dottie whispered. "That's Nicole. She's the movie star."

"You mean the statue thief," Leon said.

Casey slammed down the phone. And the three friends ran to tell Miss Duffy that they had found the phone number for Nicole and Howard Blank, the statue snatchers.

CHAPTER NINE
Shiny Badges!

Miss Duffy wasn't home so they left a note in her mailbox.

Officer Gill wasn't at the station house so they left a message with the policeman who answered the phone.

Then they went back to the clubhouse to see if there was anything else they could remember.

They were sitting and thinking when a loud knock at the door surprised them.

Two out-of-town detectives showed them their shiny badges and walked inside.

Both men were very tall. They had to duck to fit through the clubhouse door.

"Which one of you has been talking to
Nicole?" one of them asked.

"Or is it all of you?" the other man asked.

Both men had dark black hair parted on the right side. They both had pointy chins. They looked so much alike that the only way to tell them apart was that one had crooked teeth.

Dottie took out her notebook. She quickly wrote down: First-ever Calendar Club meeting with out-of-town detectives.

The man with the crooked teeth scowled. "Put that away."

"Why?" Casey asked. "Don't you want to see a picture of Nicole?" She pointed to Dottie's notebook. "There's one in there."

Both men stood up a little straighter.

"You got a picture of Nicole?" asked the one with the straight teeth.

"Why didn't you say so?" asked the man with the crooked teeth.

Dottie turned to the page with Casey's picture of the movie star. She handed the notebook to the men.

"It's a drawing," said the man with the crooked teeth. He passed it to his partner.

"They're just kids," said the partner. "Okay, kids," he said. "Listen up. We want you to forget all about this. You understand? We're handling this on our own."

"Don't you want our help?" Casey asked.

"Why would we need your help?" asked the man with the crooked teeth.

"Because we saw her," Leon said.

"We were handing out valentines," Dottie explained.

"We have a club," Casey said.

"They have a club," said the man with the straight teeth. He almost smiled. Then he decided not to. "Let's get out of here," he said to his partner.

"Don't you want to know about our club?" Casey called as they walked out the door. "Don't you want to know our plan?"

They didn't hear her. They were gone.

And they didn't care.

But Dottie cared. "What's our plan?" she asked.

"Follow me," Casey said. She ran out of the clubhouse and back to her kitchen.

Dottie and Leon followed.

This time Nicole answered the phone right away.

"I'm so sorry to bother you," said Casey. "But I thought you'd want to know."

"Want to know what?" Nicole asked.

"Another box was delivered today," Casey said. "And I think it might be another garden statue."

"Why would you think that?" Nicole asked.

"If a box was delivered with the exact same label on it, wouldn't you think it was from the exact same place?" Casey asked.

"Hold on a minute," Nicole said.

She spoke quietly to someone who was

with her. Casey strained to hear what she was saying.

"That's right," Nicole told the person. "They sent another one."

Then she spoke into the phone. "Are you still there?" she asked Casey.

"Yes," Casey said.

"Good. I need you to do me a huge favor. I need you to watch that package for me until I get there. Can you do that for me?"

"How long will it take you to get here?" Casey asked.

"Less than an hour," Nicole told her.

"Okay," Casey said.

Nicole hung up the phone without saying thank you.

"Come on!" Casey said. "She's less than an hour away!"

The three friends ran over to Miss Duffy's house. Luckily, this time she was home.

CHAPTER TEN

Scene of the Crime

Dottie, Casey, and Leon were sitting on the front steps of Miss Duffy's house when a bright red sports car squealed down the street.

It came to a sudden stop in front of them. Nicole flung open the door and rushed out.

She smiled broadly as she hurried toward them.

"Where's the box?" she asked.

"We brought it inside," Leon said.

"We were afraid it might rain," Dottie added.

They tried not to look at the sky, which was bright blue and cloudless.

But Nicole didn't seem to notice.

"Come on," Casey said. "We'll show you where we put it."

The three friends led Nicole into the house.

"Wait a minute," Nicole said, stopping in the front hall. "How did you get in here?"

"I guess you forgot to lock the door," Dottie said quickly.

"Don't worry," Leon said. "I forget to lock my door all the time."

Nicole shrugged, and followed them into the living room.

Leon stopped in front of the rock collection. "You forgot to tell me about your rocks," he said. "Can you tell me now?"

"Why don't you show me the box first," Nicole said. She started walking out of the room, to the library.

But the three friends stood, side by side, blocking her way. They crossed their arms over their chests.

"Those are your rocks, aren't they?" Casey asked.

"Sure," Nicole said. "Of course they are."

"Then why won't you tell me about them?" Leon asked. "I'd like to know about the blue one."

"That big blue one?" Nicole said. "That one is very unusual."

"What's it called?" Casey asked.

"Called?" Nicole said. "The big blue one? It's called a blue-period rock."

"I never heard of a blue-period rock before," Leon said.

Nicole smiled. "Well, now you have. Where's the box?"

The three friends didn't budge.

"How about the yellow one?" Leon asked.

"That's a yellow still-life rock," Nicole said, making it up as she went.

"I never heard of a yellow still-life rock, either," Leon said.

"We'll have to talk about that another time," Nicole said. "Where's the box?"

"I guess we'll have to talk about that another time, too," Casey said.

"Okay," said Nicole. She sounded angry. "Move out of the way. I'll find it myself."

She walked past them and right into Miss Duffy.

"Oh," said Nicole. "I didn't know you were here."

"So it's you," said Miss Duffy.

"Do you know her?" asked Casey.

"We've met," said Nicole.

"She told me she was a detective," Miss Duffy said. "She showed me her badge."

Nicole laughed. "You were very easy to fool. We had that lovely dinner together. We talked about statues for hours. And you didn't even notice when your purse disappeared for a while."

"What do you mean?" Miss Duffy asked.

"Howard was so good. He looked just like a waiter. He brought you your water and took away your purse. You had no idea. He removed your house key, made a quick copy of it, and put it back. And you never noticed a thing."

"I remember now," said Miss Duffy. "Every time I wanted to get up to go to the restroom, one of your detective friends would ask me a question and I'd sit back down."

"The twins were very good that night, too," said Nicole.

"Twins!" Dottie said.

"We met twin detectives," Leon said.

"They looked the same except one had crooked teeth," Dottie said.

"That would be Sebastian," said Nicole. "He does have awful teeth, doesn't he?"

"Where did you see those men?" Miss Duffy asked the three friends.

"They came to see us in our clubhouse," said Dottie.

"They told us they were detectives," said Leon.

"They showed us their badges," said Casey.

"I guess they fooled all of us," said Miss

Duffy. She turned to Nicole. "How did you find out the one-armed cupid was shipped here?"

"That was easy as pie," said Nicole. "It's simple to track a package if you have the shipping information. You left that in your purse, too," she told Miss Duffy. "Now, listen. Howard and I have two partners already. But we're willing to take on one more. We were just talking about how much more we could get done with a partner like you."

"Miss Duffy doesn't want to be your partner," said Dottie.

"Can we talk alone?" Nicole asked Miss Duffy.

The front door opened. They all turned as Officer Gill walked into the room.

"The only person who's going to have a talk alone with you is me," he said to Nicole.

"You can't prove anything," Nicole said, smiling.

"Maybe you should take a look outside," said Officer Gill.

He walked to the front window and opened the blinds.

Nicole looked out.

"Howard!" she exclaimed.

Dottie, Casey, Leon, and Miss Duffy looked out, too.

Two police cars were parked outside. Howard was in the back of one of them. The twins were in the back of the other.

"Howard," Nicole called out. "What happened?"

"He and those twins gave us a lot of information," said Officer Gill. "They're all going to jail. But none of them will go for quite as long as you."

He snapped a pair of handcuffs around Nicole's wrists. Then he opened the door and walked her outside.

"Howard!" Nicole yelled as they got to Officer Gill's police car. "How could you do this to me?"

But Howard just looked the other way.

Officer Gill gave the thumbs-up sign to Miss Duffy and the Calendar Club. Then he put Nicole in the back of his car with Howard. And both police cars drove away.

CHAPTER ELEVEN
A Happy Valentine's Day!

Miss Duffy sent invitations for her Valentine's Day party to everyone who lived on Daisy Lane.

She ordered lots of double-fudge brownies from Mrs. Calendar. And she ordered both real roses and chocolate ones from Dottie's uncle Eddy.

Small tables were set up throughout the house, but most of the neighbors didn't sit down. They had never been inside Miss Duffy's house before. And they wanted to look at her beautiful collections.

The party lasted several hours. Dottie,

Casey, and Leon were the last to leave.

"I have something for each of you," Miss Duffy told them as they headed toward the door.

She reached inside a bag and took out two small packages.

She gave the first one to Dottie. "This is for you," she said, "with my thanks."

Dottie carefully unwrapped the gift.

"It's a tiny cupid!" she said. She held it up and showed her friends.

"It's made out of jade," Miss Duffy explained.

She gave the other package to Casey. "Now open yours."

Casey's was almost identical. It was a smiling baby-faced cupid, carved out of pale green jade and small enough to hold in the palm of her hand.

"I found them in a flea market in Paris," said Miss Duffy. "I couldn't resist them.

They're almost exactly the same, except for their smiles."

Dottie and Casey looked closely and saw that the cupids' lopsided smiles were each slightly different.

"They're not valuable," Miss Duffy said, "but they're special to me. And I hope you'll both enjoy them."

"I love mine!" said Dottie.

"It's so cute," said Casey.

They moved closer together so they could better compare their new cupids.

Leon looked away, feeling a little left out.

"Leon," said Miss Duffy, "I have something for you, too."

His face brightened.

"It's not a cupid," she said. "I hope you don't mind."

"That's okay," said Leon. He minded, but only a little.

Miss Duffy handed Leon a package

wrapped in newspaper. It was even smaller than the packages she'd given to Dottie and Casey.

As soon as Leon unwrapped it, his eyes got wide.

"What is it?" Dottie and Casey asked together as they ran over to see.

"It's a piece of petrified wood," Miss

Duffy said. "From the Petrified Forest in Arizona."

"Look!" Leon said. His smile was so big it almost took up half his face. "Look at the shape," he told his friends.

Dottie and Casey leaned closer to see.

"Is it?" Casey asked.

"It might be," Dottie said.

"It is!" Leon said. "It's Arizona! It's petrified wood in the shape of Arizona. And it's *from* Arizona! And I got it on Valentine's Day!"

Leon was so happy that he stood up and shouted, "Happy Valentine's Day!"

And Dottie, Casey, and Miss Duffy shouted, "Happy Valentine's Day," right back.

Issue Four * Volume Four
February

Publisher: Casey Calendar
Editor: Dottie Plum
Fact Checker: Leon Spector

Calendar Club Saves Cupid!

The big news in Fruitvale this February came after Officer Gill asked the Calendar Club to keep an eye on the ivy-covered house while the woman who lived there was away.

Calendar Club members Casey Calendar, Dottie Plum, and Leon Spector weren't too happy about the request. That house was scary and it gave them the creeps!

But it was a good thing for Fruitvale! Keeping an eye on the ivy-covered house, the Calendar Club discovered a gang of clever thieves and a plot to kidnap Cupid!

In the end it was a Valentine's Day victory for the Calendar Club—and a Happy Valentine's Day for all!

DOTTIE'S WEATHER BOX

The temperature was above freezing
on February 2, 11, 12, 13, 14, and 29.
How many days was it above freezing in all?
In leap years, February has 29 days
instead of 28. Was this year a leap year?
How did you figure that out?

Weather Fun

**When it is 60 degrees in Arizona,
people put on sweaters.**

**When it is 60 degrees in Minnesota,
people put on their swim suits.**

Ask Leon

Do you have a question for Leon Spector? If you do, send it to him and he'll answer it for you. (Especially if it's about a state!)

Dear Leon,
My sister told me that Arizona is best known for being the place where they moved the London Bridge. (That's the bridge that is falling down in the song, "London Bridge is Falling Down.") I told my sister that's not true. Who's right?

From,

Please Don't Say It's My Know-it-all Sister!

Dear Please Don't Say,
I don't like to take sides, but here are the facts: London Bridge was moved to Arizona in 1968. Arizona is also known for Grand Canyon National Park, the Hoover Dam, and for being the birthplace of the first woman on the U.S. Supreme Court. So, if you're asking me, I say you're both right!

Your friend,
Leon

Leon's State Trivia

STATE BIRD: Cactus wre
STATE TREE: Paloverde
STATE FLOWER: Saguar
cactus blossom
STATE NICKNAME:
Grand Canyon State

CALENDAR CLUB — Casey Calendar

CALENDAR CLUB — Leon Spector

CALENDAR CLUB — DOTTIE PLUM

Where Is Cupid? Word Search

Cupids and words that have to do with Valentine's Day are missing. You can find the Valentine words in this puzzle.

CARDS   CHOCOLATE   CUPID   DOODAD   HEARTS
ROSES   STATUES
SWEETHEART   THIEVES   VALENTINES

```
S  R  O  S  E  S  A  O  S  T  A  T  U  H
I  P  U  C  S  E  N  I  T  N  U  L  O  V
T  H  I  E  V  E  S  P  S  D  I  P  U  C
C  H  E  C  R  S  D  O  O  E  S  W  A  I
R  A  N  T  D  V  A  E  N  T  W  E  E  O
T  T  D  R  H  A  C  A  A  S  E  D  T  A
R  S  A  S  A  L  D  R  C  S  A  E  A  E
A  C  L  T  A  E  H  I  R  D  T  H  L  O
E  E  I  E  E  N  E  E  O  T  H  T  O  A
H  S  T  V  U  T  S  O  R  T  E  E  C  D
T  D  N  E  E  I  D  T  T  N  A  E  O  T
E  D  E  I  T  N  T  C  R  V  R  W  H  S
E  I  L  H  H  E  A  R  S  A  T  S  C  E
W  D  A  T  D  S  T  A  T  U  E  S  S  S
S  T  V  T  A  S  R  O  R  O  W  H  T  H
```

85

Cupid's Crossword

ACROSS

1. A famous city in France
3. What state became a state on Valentine's Day, 1912?
5. Arizona's nickname: _____ _____ State (2 words)
6. Someone who writes articles for newspapers or magazines
8. Sweet treat given on Valentine's Day

DOWN

1. A forest of fossils in Arizona (2 words)
2. Statue with a broken arm
4. A card sent on February 14
7. Favorite flowers to give on Valentine's Day

No Two Cupids Are Alike

Miss Duffy gave Casey and Dottie almost identical cupids, except for the smiles. Here are six almost identical lines of symbols. Can you find the two lines that are exactly the same?

1) ★★✳=■==✚ ▲●□❖✺★■★★

2) ★★★=■==✚ ▼●□◆✺★■★★

3) ★★★=■==✚▼●□❖✺★■★★

4) ★★★=☆==✚▼●□❖✦★■★★

5) ★★✳=■=-✚✳★□♢✺★■★★

6) ★★★=■==✚▼●□❖✺★■★★

Valentine Rhyme Time

The answer to these definitions are two words that rhyme. Can you guess them?

1) Chocolate on Valentine's Day or any day!

_____   _____

2) Another name for Cupid's arrow

_____   _____

3) Two people who love each other but live far away

_____   _____

4) Superhero with roses

_____   _____

5) Insects' embrace

_____   _____

The Match Game

Match each state with its nickname.

Arizona	The Bay State
Louisiana	The Empire State
Tennessee	The Lone Star State
Washington	The Pelican State
Texas	The Grand Canyon State
Massachusetts	The Badger State
New York	The Volunteer State
Wisconsin	The Evergreen State

Find the Kidnapped Cupid!

Leon, Dottie, and Casey are looking for the statue thieves. Follow the trail to find the one-armed cupid!

Puzzle Answers

Dottie's Weather Box

It was above freezing six days and we know it was a leap year because one of the days that was above freezing was the 29.

Where Is Cupid? Word Search

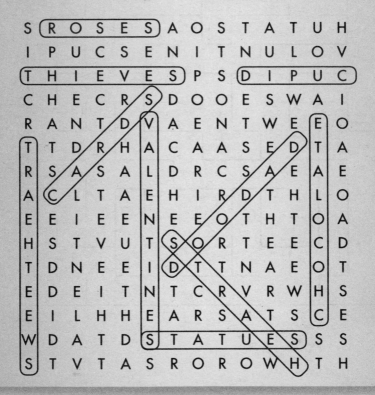

Cupid's Crossword

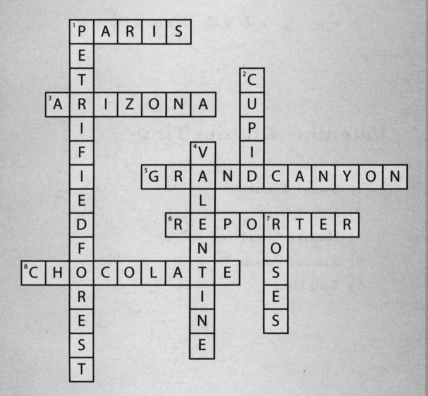

No Two Cupids Are Alike

3) ★★★=■==✚♥●□❖✺★■★★

6) ★★★=■==✚♥●□❖✺★■★★

Valentine Rhyme Time

1) Sweet Treat
2) Heart Dart
3) Hearts Apart
4) Flower Power
5) Bug Hug

The Match Game

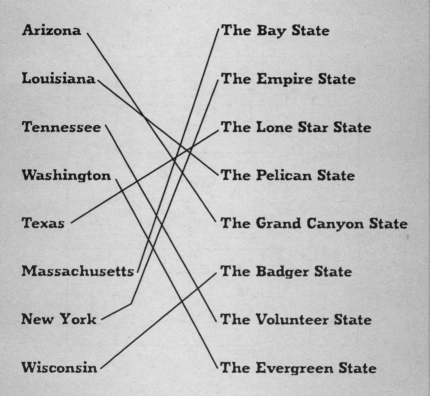

Arizona   The Bay State

Louisiana   The Empire State

Tennessee   The Lone Star State

Washington   The Pelican State

Texas   The Grand Canyon State

Massachusetts   The Badger State

New York   The Volunteer State

Wisconsin   The Evergreen State

Find the Kidnapped Cupid!

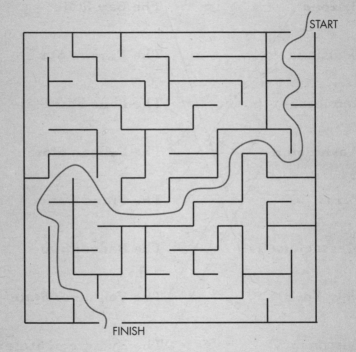

START

FINISH